DAMIAN DROOTH SUPERSLEUTH

HOW TO BE A DETECTIVE

by Barbara Mitchelhill

illustrated by Tony Ross

Librarian Reviewer
Marci Peschke
Librarian, Dallas Independent School District
MA Education Reading Specialist, Stephen F. Austin State University
Learning Resources Endorsement, Texas Women's University

Reading Consultant
Elizabeth Stedem
Educator/Consultant, Colorado Springs, CO
MA in Elementary Education, University of Denver, CO

STONE ARCH BOOKS
Minneapolis San Diego

First published in the United States in 2007
by Stone Arch Books,
151 Good Counsel Drive, P.O. Box 669,
Mankato, Minnesota 56002.
www.stonearchbooks.com

First published in 2004
by Andersen Press Ltd, London.

Library of Congress Cataloging-in-Publication Data
Mitchelhill, Barbara.
    How to Be a Detective / by Barbara Mitchelhill; illustrated by Tony
Ross.
    p. cm. — (Pathway Books) (Damian Drooth Supersleuth)
    Summary: When one of his detectives-in-training spots a woman with
nearly all of the signs of a criminal, young Damian Drooth tails her through a
dog show and learns that she really is up to no good
    ISBN-13: 978-1-59889-120-1 (hardcover)
    ISBN-10: 1-59889-120-0 (hardcover)
    ISBN-13: 978-1-59889-259-8 (paperback)
    ISBN-10: 1-59889-259-2 (paperback)
    [1. Dog shows—Fiction. 2. Cheating—Fiction. 3. Mystery and detective
stories.] I. Ross, Tony, ill. II. Title. III. Series. IV. Series: Mitchelhill, Barbara.
Damian Drooth Supersleuth.
PZ7.M697How 2007
[Fic]—dc22   2006007180

Art Director: Heather Kindseth
Graphic Designer: Kay Fraser

1 2 3 4 5 6 11 10 09 08 07 06

Printed in the United States of America.

jmys
mit

b17391568

Table of Contents

Chapter 1

My name is Damian Drooth and I'm a very successful detective. You might have heard of me. I've solved lots of crimes in our town.

Not long ago, I decided that there must be millions of kids who wanted to learn to be crime busters like me. So I put up a sign at the school playground that read:

Damian Drooth, Famous Detective and Supersleuth, will give a talk on how to spot Crooks and Thieves and Criminals.

> Come to the shed in my garden at
> 10 o'clock on Saturday morning.
> Wear sunglasses. Do not be late.
> Entrance fee: 1 bag of chips.

I picked Saturday because Mom was working that day. She has a business called Home Cooking Unlimited. She makes cakes and sandwiches and takes them to weddings and parties. She likes to keep busy. I think she gets bored just hanging around the house.

On Saturday she was doing the food at a flower show. Sometimes I go along and help, but I don't really like flowers.

"I'll stay home and do my homework," I said. "I have a really interesting report to do for history."

Mom tightened her lips and squinted her eyes. That is her suspicious look.

"That doesn't sound like you, Damian," she said. "What are you up to?"

I didn't say anything. I just stood there looking hurt. But it did the trick.

In the end, she said, "All right. But you have to stay in the house. I'll ask Mrs. Robertson next door to stop by and keep an eye on you."

Of course I agreed. If I hadn't, I would have spent Saturday at the flower show cleaning up the tables and listening to people talk about fertilizer.

Chapter 2

On Saturday morning, Mom was late loading the van. I was almost finished with my breakfast and she was still running in and out of the kitchen. In a rush, as usual.

"Can you carry something out for me, Damian?" she panted.

"Okay," I said. I put down my toast and picked up a chocolate cake. My favorite.

"No, not that," said Mom and grabbed it from me. "Carry the silverware."

So I did. But even this didn't make her happy. Okay, so I dropped the box, but nothing was broken and I picked up every last knife and fork.

Except the ones that fell down the drain.

Mom finally drove off at nine o'clock.

The kids arrived for the Detective School an hour later. They formed a long line outside the garden shed. I could tell they were excited to learn.

Todd Browning and his sister, Lavender, were at the front of the line. So they got the only seats.

I collected the entrance fees (seven bags of chips in all), which I stashed away in a box. Then I stood up on a bucket to give my first talk.

"Okay," I said. "I'm glad that you've got your notebooks and pencils. Every good detective should have them."

Then, to impress the kids, I didn't have to say a thing. I just got out my press clips from the local paper.

YOUNG GIRL SAVED !

Police were astonished when a young boy, **Damian Drooth**, saved the young daughter of a film director kidnapped by an international crook.

HOUSE STARTED FIRE

DIAMOND FOUND !

A diamond necklace belonging to a pop star was recovered by a local boy detective. **Damian Drooth** was guarding presents worth thousands of dollars at the wedding of the famous pop star Tiger Lilly to soccer player Gary Blaze.

I could tell they were shocked by my fame. Then they started asking questions.

"Don't the police get mad because you're smarter than they are?"

"Did any criminals pay you big money to stop you from telling on them?"

That kind of thing.

Lavender Browning, who was only a little kid, asked me, "What's it like to be famous, Damian?"

"Yeah, tell us," the rest shouted.

But I was too modest to answer. Instead, I began to explain my Theories of Criminal Detection. After all, the kids were there to learn.

"These are the most common types of crooks you're likely to spot," I said as I hung two posters I had drawn on the wall.

Criminal Type NO.1

Eyes set close together (A good example is Mr. Forrester in fourth grade. Watch out for him!)

Criminal Type NO. 2

Anybody with a beard (usually men).
Black beards are the worst.
(Take a look at the new crossing guard
at school. He could be up to no good.
Only time will tell!)

Some of the kids were scribbling in their notebooks. Some of them were yawning from all the listening and learning. I feel just like that in Mr. Johnson's math class.

"Always remember," I said, "the best way to track down criminals is to be alert."

"How do we do that, Damian?" Harry Houseman called out.

I explained. "If we went down to Main Street and stayed alert, we'd probably spot a criminal."

"Then let's do it!" said Todd.

I shook my head. "Not today."

The fact was, I was secretly looking forward to eating the chips before Mom came home. I'd promised to stay in the house, and I always keep my promises. Almost always.

"Come on, Damian," shouted Winston Hunt. "What are you scared of?"

"Yeah!" called out one of the girls. "Show us how it's done. If you can."

Then everybody started talking. There was almost a riot. They were so excited. How could I refuse? So we headed to Main Street.

Chapter 3

"Just remember what I told you,"
I said when we reached Main Street.
"Look out for the common types of
crooks. Check your notes, if you need to."

We were just passing the bookstore
when Lavender tugged at my sleeve.

"Over there, Damian. Look! A
criminal!" she said.

A man with a beard was riding on
a scooter along the sidewalk. His beard
was white, so he probably wasn't a
major criminal.

"Mmm," I said. "Maybe he is, or maybe not."

Lavender, who got easily excited, was convinced. "He's a robber!" she cried. "He's going to mug somebody and take their money. I can tell."

"Okay. Okay. Maybe he is a robber," I said. "Everyone, if you have any money, hold onto it. Muggers can be very sneaky. I'll show you how to keep a close watch on him. Follow me."

I pressed my back up against the wall, my cap pulled over my eyes.

All the other kids did the same. We kept our eyes glued to the suspect as he came down Main Street. Then he started heading toward a woman who was collecting for charity. And the can she was holding was full of money!

"He's going to steal it!" said Lavender. "What can we do?"

Harry couldn't wait to help. "Don't worry, Lavender! I'll stop him!" He darted forward between the scooter and the charity collector. He stopped, held his hand in the air, and then shouted, "Stop right there!"

The man on the scooter was shocked. He tried to swerve to avoid Harry. Maybe he was making a getaway. I don't know. The scooter tipped over and the man went sprawling on the sidewalk.

He never got his hands on the collection money.

Seconds later, there were crowds of people around him. He had no chance of getting away.

Another job well done.

"Come on," I called to Harry. "Never stay on the scene of the crime once you've solved it."

Chapter 4

Things were going well, but they looked even better when I had a great idea.

"I want to try out a new theory," I said. "You can all come with me if you want."

"Okay, Damian," said Lavender. "Where are we going?"

"The library," I said. "We can do some people-watching without anybody noticing us."

The theory I was working on was this: people with thin lips were more likely to be crooks. Stealing jewels and breaking into banks. That kind of thing.

I had my theory after looking at the photos in the local paper. Going into the library would give me the chance to see if my theory was true.

So we walked in, took some books off the shelves, and sat at the tables. Of course, everybody thought we were reading, but we weren't. We were peering over the tops of the books, looking for criminals.

We watched for at least ten minutes and then Lavender hissed, "Pssst!" She was trying to get my attention.

She was pointing at the librarian's desk where a large woman with a fur coat and blonde hair was checking out a book. "I think that's one," she whispered.

I got up and crept over to the desk, hoping no one would notice. The other kids followed. When I got near, I could see that the woman was borrowing a suspicious book called "Loot."

(Detectives know that loot is a crook's word for stolen things.)

This was not the only suspicious thing. The woman's eyes were close together, but they were hidden by glasses.

Even better, her lips were thin and tight and there were little wrinkles around them. Bingo! She was an excellent example of all my Criminal Types (except she didn't have a beard).

I turned to Lavender and gave her a thumbs-up. The kid might be a great detective one day.

We were getting funny looks from Miss Travis, the librarian. I don't know why. She is usually very understanding. She must have had a headache.

The blonde woman put the book in her bag and was ready to go. As she turned and headed for the door, I gave a signal for the others to follow. But at this point, my luck changed.

"Damian!" Miss Travis called. "Will you and your friends please put away those books before you leave?"

I gritted my teeth and gave her one of my best smiles.

"We'll do it later," I said. "We've just got to—"

"Now!" she shouted.

Miss Travis never shouts. I guess she wasn't feeling well.

We rushed over to the table, stuck the books back on the shelves, and dashed out of the library. Main Street was crowded with shoppers. I wondered if I'd lost the thin-lipped woman forever.

"There she is!" said Harry, who was so tall he could see over people's heads. "She's by that white van."

She stood out from the crowd with her big blonde hair and fur coat. We chased her down Main Street, but people kept crashing into us.

"Keep your eyes on her," I said. "We need to know what she's up to."

Before we could catch her, she turned into the Historical Society.

"We've got to stop her," I said. "She's probably doing a raid."

It was terrible luck that, at that moment, I bumped into Mr. Robertson from next door.

"Hey, hey, hey, Damian," he said, grabbing my shoulders. "What are you doing in town? Your mother said you were staying home today."

I didn't know what to say.

"You'd better come with me," he said. "My wife will be worried silly, wondering where you are."

I looked around at the training detectives. "Sorry, guys. Something's turned up. I've got to go," I said.

Now we'd never find out about the blonde woman with the thin lips.

Chapter 5

When Mom came home, I could tell she had a tough day. She looked really stressed.

"I got two calls on my cell phone," she said. "One from Sue Greenspan, who was collecting for charity. And one from Miss Travis at the library."

She glared at me. "Why were you running through town this morning with a gang of hooligans? Knocking down old people and wrecking the library! Can't I trust you for half a day, Damian?"

I hate it when she shouts.

"Tomorrow," she said, "you're coming with me, like it or not. I'm catering at the local dog show and I'm not leaving you behind to get into more trouble. You can watch the dogs."

Actually, I like dogs. So the dog show sounded good.

I made quick phone calls to the kids who had come to the Detective School that morning.

"Be at the County Exhibition Hall by ten o'clock tomorrow for another training session," I told them. "Bring a dog if you have one." I figured that no one would suspect kids with dogs were working as undercover trainee detectives.

By the time I arrived with Mom, the dog show was in full swing. I offered to help carry the food from the van, but she wouldn't let me.

"I'll manage by myself, thank you, Damian," she said. "It's safer."

So I left her alone and went and settled into a seat.

Todd and Lavender had already arrived with their dog, Curly. Winston walked in soon after with Thumper, who smelled really bad.

"Harry's coming later," he said, "but I don't think anyone else wants to hunt for crooks on a Sunday."

"Their loss," I said. "They'll never make the grade without practice."

At this point, Lavender started tugging at my sleeve in a worried kind of way.

"Damian!" she said. "I saw her!"

"Who did you see?" I asked.

"That blonde woman with the thin lips. The one planning to rob the Historical Society."

I took out my shades and put them on. At once, I was alert and ready for action.

"Over there!" said Lavender, pointing her finger. "She's right in the middle of the ring! Look! She's the judge!"

I could hardly believe it. The blonde was there, all right. It was my chance to catch a crook red-handed. Not to mention a chance to prove my Criminal Theory number 3.

Here are the lists I made:

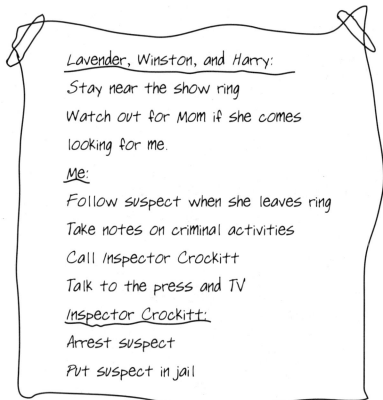

Lavender, Winston, and Harry:

Stay near the show ring

Watch out for Mom if she comes looking for me.

Me:

Follow suspect when she leaves ring

Take notes on criminal activities

Call Inspector Crockitt

Talk to the press and TV

Inspector Crockitt:

Arrest suspect

Put suspect in jail

We all watched while the blonde woman judged the Small Dog competition. First she looked at one dog. Then the next. It took forever to check them all.

When she finally announced the winner, I was disgusted. The winner had hair down to its feet and a stupid red bow on its head. It was owned by someone named Major Dalrymple. How would he like it if someone tied a bow in his hair (if he had any)?

She gave him a silver cup and a certificate and then walked out of the ring.

"Okay," I said. "I'm going to follow her. See what information I can get."

I needed more facts if I was going to call the police and have her arrested.

"Take Curly with you," said Lavender. "She's a good guard dog with big teeth!"

I shrugged. I didn't need protection. I'm used to danger.

Lavender insisted. "You might get into a really tricky situation."

Just to make Lavender happy, I took Curly along.

Outside the hall, I spotted the judge heading toward the refreshment room. The only problem was, Mom was in the room, too.

I needed a disguise. There was a small changing room nearby and I found a large hat and a coat that sort of fit me, sort of. Not even my own mother would recognize me.

I went into the refreshment room, tied Curly to a table leg, and began to observe the blonde woman.

Activities of Criminal Blonde Woman.
Puts 3 teaspoons of sugar in coffee.
Drinks coffee.
Opens bag
Takes roll of money out of bag
And counts it !!!!!!!!!!
Does this mean she did the raid on
The Historical Society?
Probably !!!!!!!!!!

Just as I finished writing my notes, I saw Mom come out of the kitchen. She was carrying one of her chocolate cakes (my favorite). It was too much for me to watch.

Even the best detectives need a break sometimes.

I decided that if I went up to the counter with my head down, I could buy a slice of cake and she'd never notice. But I forgot about Curly. She decided to follow me, dragging the table with her and wrapping her leash around a waiter's legs.

"Hey!" he said (very rudely, I thought). "You can't bring dogs in here. You'll have to take him out."

"It's a girl, actually," I said.

At the sound of my voice, Mom looked up.

"Damian?" she said. "What are you doing here? I told you to go and watch the show."

"Sorry, Mom," I said. "I felt dizzy.
I thought a piece of your cake would
make me feel better."

She could have looked more
sympathetic, but anyway, she cut a
giant slice and put it on a paper plate.

"Go back to the show," she said, "and take that heap of hair with you." She meant Curly.

"Okay, Mom," I said.

I began to walk away. I had the cake in one hand and Curly's leash in the other hand.

"And for goodness sake, take off that ridiculous coat!" she called after me.

She didn't realize I was in disguise. It's tough working undercover.

During all the fuss with Mom and the waiter, I had taken my eyes off the blonde woman.

Big mistake! When I glanced over at her table, she was gone.

Maybe she suspected that I was watching her. Maybe she made a run for it. It didn't matter. I wasn't going to let her get away.

Chapter 6

When I got back to the show, Lavender amazed me once again with her powers of detection.

She looked at me and said, "I can see you've been eating some chocolate cake, Damian."

How did she guess? The kid must be a genius!

Unfortunately, I had to tell her that our suspect escaped. "Once they know you're on to them," I said, "things can get really tough."

Lavender looked puzzled. "But isn't that her?" she said, pointing to the far side of the ring, toward the last row of seats. The suspect was standing there talking to someone.

"You've got laser eyes," said Harry.

"Yeah!" said Winston. "Good job, Lavender."

"Nice," said Todd.

I wasn't too excited. There was real detective work still to be done, and I was going to do it.

"Okay," I said. "I'm going to sneak over there."

"But she might see you, Damian!" said Lavender.

"Don't worry, Lavender. Nobody will see me. I can be almost invisible when I need to be. Watch and learn," I said.

I had practiced being invisible in the kitchen, down the halls at school, and in the movie theater. I had studied for months. Now was my chance to put it to use in preventing crime.

I dropped down flat onto the floor.

Slowly, I moved forward keeping my body in contact with the ground, like a soldier in the army. It was not easy.

When I got to the other side, the blonde woman was still there, talking to a man who looked familiar.

I hid under a seat in the back row.

Then I pressed my ear to the ground and listened.

". . . wasn't enough money . . ."

"The risk is too great . . ."

". . . greedy . . ."

". . . plan carefully . . ."

I couldn't hear every word because Curly had followed me and was stuffing her nose in my face. I tried to push her away, but she started whining and letting everyone know where I was!

I might not have heard everything the blonde woman said, but I heard enough. It was obvious that she was discussing the Historical Society.

I headed back with Curly, to tell the others. "They're planning a robbery," I said as I sat down. "I've seen that man she's talking to before. I think he works at the Historical Society."

"Typical," said Winston. "He's in on it." I nodded wisely.

"Aha! He's a crook, too!" said Lavender. "You've got to stop them, Damian." She trusted me. I had to act fast.

"Lend me your cell phone, Lavender," I said. "I'm going to call Inspector Crockitt."

Chapter 7

I left a message for the Inspector. It was perfectly clear. "Come quick and arrest the judge at the Dog Show who is a dangerous bank robber."

But the police can be very slow. A whole hour passed and no one came.

Maybe the desk sergeant I spoke to hadn't written it down correctly. Maybe he hadn't given the message to Inspector Crockitt.

"Funny," I said to the others. "I thought he'd be here right away."

"I don't think the police are coming," said Harry. "We're running out of time. The dog show's almost over."

Harry was right. The Large Dog competition was the last in the show. Our suspect was about to award the cup to the winner. Soon, I'd have to go home with Mom and another criminal would have escaped.

Suddenly, Winston stood up in his seat and pointed. "Hey! Look who's got the cup," he said. "It's that major who won the other competition."

Winston had obviously learned my lessons about staying alert.

"That's not a major," I said, staring into the ring. "He's the judge's partner in crime. They're planning a robbery. I heard them talking."

"Oh no!" said Winston. "Then we've got to act now. We can't wait for the police."

"What should we do, Damian?" Lavender asked.

I thought about it.

Then I gave the kids instructions for simple things to do. I would handle the dangerous stuff myself.

This is what happened.

I ran into the center of the show ring. Hundreds of pairs of eyes were on me, but I didn't care.

The dog show judge (our suspect) looked horrified.

"Get out of the ring!" she shouted. "You're ruining the contest."

But I refused to move. Instead, I turned to the people in the middle of the show ring who were standing with their dogs.

"This judge is a criminal," I said. "She's a thief."

At that moment, the blonde woman ran for the exit, and so did the major. It was just what I expected.

But I was ready for them. I gave
the signal to my trainee detectives
and they released their dogs shouting,
"Go, go, go!" Then Curly and Thumper
chased after the two crooks.

"Aaaahhhhggg!" screamed the
blonde as she tripped over a loose piece
of carpet.

"Noooooo!" yelled the major as he
tripped over the blonde.

"Woof, woof, woof!" barked the dogs as they landed on top of the two crooks.

The dogs in the competition joined in. They barked and yelped and jumped around. It was amazing!

Security guards came, shouting, "Get those dogs off! They're dangerous!"

I stood there, watching. I had solved another crime. I had punished another crook. But it didn't turn out how I planned. I suddenly found myself in the grip of a huge security guard. I was furious.

"What are you doing?" I demanded. "Don't you know who I am?"

"You're the one who caused this riot," he said.

I was shocked. "But that lady is the one you should be arresting," I said.

I pointed to a leg sticking out from the pile of excited dogs.

The security guards didn't seem to know what to do. By the time Inspector Crockitt arrived, our suspects were still stuck and calling for help.

It was only when four police officers managed to pull the dogs off, that the criminals emerged, shaking and terrified.

"I confess, I confess," said the judge.

Now that was what I wanted to hear.

The next day, there were big headlines in the local paper.

All the kids at school gathered around to read it.

DAMIAN DOES IT AGAIN

Dog Show Judge Heads For Jail.

"You're a brilliant detective," said Lavender, looking at me.

"Yeah," said Winston. "I can't believe you caught a bank robber like that."

It was good to feel appreciated. But then Harry decided to read every word of the article.

"Wait a minute," he said when he was done. "It doesn't mention a bank robbery here. Or a Historical Society, for that matter."

I shrugged. "So?"

"It says that the judge was being paid by the major to give his dogs the award."

Harry smirked and put down the paper. "You were just lucky, Damian."

Did it matter? I had solved a crime, hadn't I?

"Well, I think," said Lavender, "cheating at competitions is just as bad as robbing banks. Don't you know that the major could sell puppies for lots of money if their parents were prize winners?"

Of course I knew that. But I didn't say anything. I just nodded.

The following week, Inspector Crockitt came to school to talk about my part in solving the crime. He went on and on about not doing dangerous things and about finding an adult when we're in trouble. All basic stuff really. I'd heard it lots of times.

Before he left, the Inspector wanted to have a word with me. He likes to pick up tips on how to solve crimes. I suggested that the police should speed up their response time.

"You got to the dog show hours after I left the message for you," I said.

"Sorry, Damian," he replied. "I thought it was a joke."

"A joke?" I said.

"Yes, I wasn't sure the message was from you," he said.

I almost choked. Is that how they run the police department?

After that, I figured out how to avoid mistakes like that in the future. I wrote to Inspector Crockitt and told him about my idea for a secret code. Only the two of us will know about it. I will be able to send messages about criminals to him. It's a great idea and I think he'll be really pleased.

I'm still waiting for a reply.

About the Author

Barbara Mitchelhill started writing when she was seven years old. She says, "When I was eight or nine, I used to pretend I was a detective, just like Damian. My friend, Liz, and I used to watch people walking down our street and we would write clues in our notebooks. I don't remember catching any criminals!" She has written many books for children. She lives in Shropshire, England, and gets some of her story ideas when she walks her dogs, Jeff and Ella.

About the Illustrator

Tony Ross was born in London in 1938. He has illustrated lots of books, including some by Paula Danziger, Michael Palin, and Roald Dahl. He also writes and illustrates his own books. He has worked as a cartoonist, graphic designer, and art director of an advertising agency. When he was a kid, he wanted to grow up to be a cowboy.

Glossary

astonish (uh-STON-ish)—to amaze

charity (CHA-ruh-tee)—a group that is organized to help the poor or needy

detective (di-TEK-tive)—someone whose work is trying to solve crimes

disguise (diss-GIZE)—something that changes or hides a person's appearance

fertilizer (FUR-tuh-lize-er)—a substance added to soil to make it better for growing plants

greedy (GREE-dee)—wanting all one can get

modest (MOD-ist)—not too boastful

mug (MUHG)—to rob

raid (RAYD)—a sudden attack

sleuth (SLOOTH)—a detective

suspect (suh-SPEKT)—to think someone is guilty

suspicious (suh-SPISH-uhss)—to think or feel that something may be wrong

sympathetic (sim-puh-THEH-tik)—understanding another's feelings or ideas

Discussion Questions

1. Damian mentions and uses three "Theories of Criminal Detection." What are they? Do you agree or disagree with them? Explain your thinking.

2. What do you think are the characteristics of a criminal? Discuss your thinking.

3. When Damian tells his mother that he wants to stay home and work on a report for school, she says to him on page 8 "that doesn't sound like you." What does she mean by this? Was she right or wrong?

Writing Prompts

1. Damian teaches his friends how to be detectives. Write about what you could teach your friends. Include how you would go about teaching them.

2. What do Damian's actions show about his character? Should he have gone with his friends to Main Street or stayed home as he promised? Explain.

3. Detectives need to be alert. Was there a time when you were alert and saw or heard something that other people missed? Did you try to tell them? Did they believe you? Write and explain what happened.

Internet Sites

Do you want to know more about subjects related to this book? Or are you interested in learning about other topics? Then check out FactHound, a fun, easy way to find Internet sites.

Our investigative staff has already sniffed out great sites for you!

Here's how to use FactHound:

1. Visit *www.facthound.com*

2. Select your grade level.

3. To learn more about subjects related to this book, type in the book's ISBN number: **1598891200**.

4. Click the **Fetch It** button.

FactHound will fetch the best Internet sites for you!